hates chris™

Everybody Hates

First
Girlfriends

by Felicia Pride

Simon Spotlight
New York   London   Toronto   Sydney

Based on the TV series *Everybody Hates Chris*™ as seen on The CW

SIMON SPOTLIGHT
An imprint of Simon & Schuster Children's Publishing Division
1230 Avenue of the Americas, New York, New York 10020
TM and © 2007 CBS Studios Inc. All Rights Reserved.
All rights reserved, including the right of reproduction in whole or in part in any form.
SIMON SPOTLIGHT and colophon are registered trademarks of Simon & Schuster, Inc.
Manufactured in the United States of America
First Edition 10 9 8 7 6 5 4 3 2 1
ISBN-13: 978-1-4169-3798-2
ISBN-10: 1-4169-3798-6
Library of Congress Catalog Card Number 2007927181

Chapter 1

"I can't believe you missed the game of the season. It was incredible!" I said, as Greg and I walked toward our lockers.

I started reenacting the last moments of the game for him. "Ten seconds left. The Knicks are down by three. Bernard King has the ball. He fakes, turns, and hits a three-point shot." I threw my hands in the air like I'd just made a basket. "*All* net. Ties the game.

"Two seconds left," I continued. "Knicks have the ball and now they're down by two. The crowd is on the edge of their seats. It's *so* intense."

"The ball is passed to King. He does a quick fake, runs down the clock, and *boom*, he lands another three-point shot. The crowd roars and the Knicks reign supreme!" As I released my air ball to shoot the winning basket, I rammed right into the school bully, Joey Caruso. "Oof!"

When I turned around, my archnemesis, the redheaded terror whose life's mission was to torment me, was on the floor. He was stunned. My mouth was hanging open, and Greg looked like he was about to wet his pants. This was not the way I wanted to start my week.

Then, just as I was about to mutter some sort of apology to stall the butt-kicking that would be coming my way, Teresa Johnson ran up to me and gave me a big hug. I managed a half smile as she nearly squeezed the life out of me.

4

What was she doing here? Usually I'd welcome this type of attention from a girl, but this was Teresa Johnson, and I cringed. Since we were children, Teresa has had this thing for me, and I have never been sure why. Maybe I'm some sort of challenge. But she has always followed me around Brooklyn, pops up at my house unexpectedly, and calls me all the time. She definitely tops Tonya in being the most annoying female I know. There are many days when I hide behind garbage cans to avoid her. And I thought I was going to be free from her when I started going to Corleone Jr. High, on the other side of Brooklyn, far away from our Bed-Stuy neighborhood. But somehow she's managed to find her way here, too!

"You saved me," Teresa said. "You're my Prince Charming." Obviously her version of what had happened was quite different from reality. She thought I'd knocked Joey down on purpose.

Then, before I knew it, a crowd started forming

around us. Uh-oh. This was bad.

"You saw that guy harassing me and you came to my rescue," Teresa went on. "You were jealous, weren't you? I always knew you liked me. You were just playing hard to get."

I couldn't believe what I was hearing—and that half the school was hearing it too! Could this day get any worse?

Then a voice came from the floor. "Chris, you're dead meat. I'm going to get you for this." Oh, yeah. I still had to deal with Joey.

Usually I would be up and running by now, but that would be pointless. If I admitted that I hadn't been protecting Teresa, everyone would know that defeating Joey was a fluke. And for the first time, it felt good to be the one in control instead of the other way around. I decided to take advantage of being in the position of power.

"Yeah, sure you're going to get me back," I told Joey in a fake brave voice. "You don't want any more of this." The crowd roared, and I felt like I really had made the winning shot, even though I was shaking inside. I looked desperately over at Greg, and he cocked his head toward the classrooms. It was probably a good idea to move on before Joey got up and called my bluff. Teresa whispered in my ear that she'd see her cute prince later.

I was never so eager to get to class.

During my next three classes, all I could think about was how Teresa managed to follow me to this school. I started to see her face in the strangest places. When I opened my history book, there she was grinning back at me. When I looked at the poster of the planets in science class, there was her face in place of Saturn. When I screamed, Mr. Burke yelled at me. I knew it was a sign of bad things to come.

Chapter 2

At lunch Greg was eager to hear about the mystery girl I'd saved.

"That's Teresa," I said flatly. "She and I kind of grew up together in Bed-Stuy. Our moms are friends. We always went to the same schools. Ever since I can remember she's liked me, but not in a good way. She's more like a stalker. I thought I'd be safe here, but—"

Suddenly Teresa was in my face. She was so quick and sneaky, kind of like a roach. I jumped back to avoid being mowed down.

"I can't thank you enough for saving my life," she exclaimed. She gave me one of those girlie looks.

"Uh, I didn't save your life, Teresa," I replied, hoping she sensed the irritation in my voice.

"Oh, you're so modest, Chris. That's why I like you." Her tone was the same one my mother used when she wanted my father to buy her something.

"How did you end up at Corleone?" I asked. I hoped she would say she was on some sort of one-day exchange program and that tomorrow she'd be returning to her school in Bed-Stuy.

"I told my mother how well you were doing here, and she thought I could benefit from coming too," she said with a smirk. Then she looked at Greg. "Are you going to introduce me to your friend?"

"Oh, Teresa, this is Greg. Greg, this is Teresa," I said quickly.

"Any friend of Chris's is a friend of mine," Teresa told him.

"I feel the same way," said Greg with a grin. I hoped he could see the stalker inside her.

Teresa turned back to me. "Will my hero buy me lunch?" she asked.

"I only have enough money for myself," I answered.

"And you would sacrifice your hunger for me? You are such a gentleman," she responded, completely suckering me! But I didn't want her to cause a scene. People were already thinking that she was my girlfriend. So I pulled out my last bit of change and bought her lunch. I hoped that now she would leave me alone.

"Thank you, cutie. I'll be waiting at the table for you," said Teresa.

"Dude!" Greg cried excitedly. "You've got a girlfriend. High five!" He held up his hand, but I refused to return the slap. I was frustrated and hungry.

"She's not my girlfriend!" I snapped.

"Does she know that she's not your girlfriend?"

he asked. We looked over to Teresa, and she blew me a kiss. I ducked quickly to make sure that it didn't hit me.

"She seems like a nice girl, and she has a cute face," Greg added. "Most importantly, she likes you. Isn't she the first girl to do that?"

Greg had a point. Teresa was far from hideous-looking. She was copper-toned, like the pennies in the coin collection I used to own before my father found it and used it to buy groceries. And her black hair always looked fresh. It was obvious that she combed it every day. It was just my luck that the first girl to take a serious interest in me filled me with dread. She scared me—not with her looks, but with her personality. I had to find a way to get out of being the object of her attention.

When we reached the table, Teresa motioned for me to sit in the chair next to her.

"You know, Chris," she said. "I was just minding my business when that boy Joey came up to me.

Do you know what he said to me?"

"No."

"He said he figured that I was new and he could show me around if I wanted. He asked me my name and told me I was pretty."

I couldn't believe that Joey was so bold with girls. That was the first time I ever thought that I needed to be more like him.

"I was about to tell him that I already had a honey who went to this school and that he should back off— and that's when you plowed into him! Your timing was perfect."

I looked at Greg, and he stared into his plastic-looking lasagna. He wasn't going to help me out of this one.

"Well, actually what really happened—" I started to say, but she didn't let me explain.

"No one has ever rescued me like that. It was really romantic."

"But it wasn't—"

"I mean, I felt like a real princess and that you were my knight in shining armor."

"Teresa, I was just reenacting the—"

"You know, everyone in the neighborhood is wrong about you. You're not a punk, you're my fierce warrior. Wait until I tell everyone how you saved me."

Well, maybe I could let her believe that I saved her. What harm could there be? Maybe it would even improve my reputation. So I stopped trying to interrupt her. I just let her talk on and on about my bravery. Greg looked like he was going to puke in his lasagna, but I felt like the black Superman. Clark Kent really had nothing on me.

The entire day passed with no sign of Joey Caruso. Trust me, I was really watching my back, too. At any moment he could jump out from an empty class-room and catch me off guard. He wasn't going to let me get away with embarrassing him in front of half the school. Maybe I should be grateful to Teresa.

Maybe it was what she did that saved me from getting a beating from Joey this morning.

On the bus ride home, I grabbed the seat next to a kid in my science class I never talked to. Then Teresa got on the bus, and I was happy that she wouldn't be able to sit with me. But I was wrong. Teresa asked my classmate to move so that she could sit with her "boyfriend." He got up without any objections. If I had the money, I would have bribed him to stay.

The ride turned out to be the longest journey of my life. For more than an hour, Teresa talked about how long she'd waited for the day that we would make our feelings for each other official. I held my head down and rubbed my forehead, hoping that a brilliant plan would emerge. Or maybe I'd disappear.

I couldn't hurt her feelings or be mean. But more so, Teresa had managed to do the unthinkable: win my mother's heart. Over the years of coming over and calling my house, Teresa has formed a daughterlike bond with my mom. And once my mother found out that we had a "relationship," it would be near impossible to get out of it.

"I can't wait to tell your mother," Teresa said, like she'd heard my thoughts. "She's going to be just as excited as we are!" She laid her head on my shoulder. I pretended that I had a tic so she'd remove it, but that didn't work.

"About the boyfriend thing," I began, trying to let her down easily.

"What?" she asked. From my tone, she could tell it wasn't good news. Instant tears formed in her eyes.

All I could hear was my mother's voice. "Boy, what's wrong with you? How dare you break Teresa's heart! What did she ever do to you?"

"Uh," I stalled. Then, instead of saying, "I don't think we will work out," I blurted out, "When do you want to go out?" The words just fell out of my mouth. I kicked myself inside, hard.

For the remainder of the ride, Teresa talked with her head firmly planted on my shoulder.

"Remember when . . . ," she said so many times that I started to tune her out. Instead I concentrated on coming up with a plan to keep this "relationship" a secret until I could think of a way to get out of it.

When we got off the bus, she insisted, "Let me walk home with you to tell your mother the good news."

"My mother isn't home," I said quickly. "We can tell her another day."

"Well, I'll still walk my handsome hunk home."

Handsome hunk? Where does she come up with this stuff? I walked fast, but Teresa kept up. We reached my house in record time.

"Well, uh, see you later." I turned around quickly to walk up the stairs, but Teresa grabbed me and spun me around. I'd never realized she was so strong.

"Until we see each other again, my love," she said, before planting a wet kiss on my cheek and walking away backward while staring at me—and she didn't even trip or bump into anything! I shook my head, not sure what I had done to deserve this.

I ran into the house to find Drew and Tonya waiting for me with huge smiles on their faces. "Chris and Teresa sitting in a tree, k-i-s-s-i-n-g," they sang in unison.

"I'm going to tell Mom you and Teresa were playing kissy-face," Tonya teased. So much for keeping the whole thing a secret.

"You can't tell Mom," I pleaded.

"Well, what are you going to give me?" my sister asked. She was the queen of bribery. So young, yet so cunning. I hoped she wasn't going to make a career out of it. But for now I promised to buy her candy in exchange for her silence.

Drew congratulated me. "Bro, you finally got yourself a girlfriend." He patted me on the back like a proud father. "I didn't think this day would come. Let me know if you ever need advice about women."

Chapter 3

That night at dinner I was nervous that Tonya would sell me out. I looked over at her and she was gleaming with excitement, like she was going to explode at any moment. Drew still had that congratulatory look on his face. I couldn't even enjoy the macaroni and cheese or baked chicken.

"How was school today?" my mother asked us.

Drew and Tonya waited for me to answer.

"It was fine," I said.

"You're going to eat those greens, right?" my father asked. I looked down at my plate. I had two string beans on it. Two too many left for my father. I stuffed them into my mouth.

"So what did you do in school today?" my mother persisted.

I was about to answer when the phone rang. "Who is that calling at dinnertime?" Mom wondered, annoyed. "They should know better than to disturb us while we're eating." I thought for sure she was going to lay out whoever was on the other end, but her voice softened when she started talking.

"Well, we just started eating, but we always have room for you, sweetheart. See you soon."

"Who was that?" my father asked when she hung up the phone. He was concerned that we were going to give away precious food.

"Oh, it was Teresa, Jackie's daughter. She's coming over for dinner."

I almost spat out my macaroni and cheese.

I didn't even see this one coming! What was I going to do?

"Why?" asked Dad. He didn't like to feed any extra mouths, no matter who they were. Even when his brother came to visit he kept a tally of how much food he ate.

Tonya couldn't hold it in. "Because she's Chris's girlfriend," she blurted. "They were playing kissy-face today after school." She looked so relieved to have finally released the juicy information.

I was madder than the time I lost to a seven-year-old at the arcade. "We were not!" I shouted, before mouthing "No candy" to Tonya.

"Chris, don't yell at your sister!" my mother exclaimed. Then she started to gush over me.

"My baby has his first girlfriend? Jackie and I always said you two would eventually get together. But I never thought it would be so soon."

"Just like his father, good with the ladies," said Dad with a wink.

Mom just rolled her eyes. "Remember, Julius, our first date? And how you ruined it?"

It was obvious my father didn't want to revisit the past. "Woman, how many times do I have to apologize for that? It was years ago," he said in an exasperated voice.

"Just because it was years ago doesn't mean I've gotten over it," Mom told him. "A first date is supposed to be special, not a nightmare. You remember that, Chris."

Wait a minute—how did I get involved in this?

"What happened?" Tonya asked.

"Go ahead, Julius, tell your daughter what happened."

My father studied his plate. "Uh, I'd rather not."

"See! It was so terrible that you don't even want to talk about it with your children."

"Rochelle, I don't want to argue over something that happened so long ago. Yes, I ruined our first date. I know that. But I'm tired of apologizing for it. Let me make it right once and for all. What if I take you on a second first date to replace the bad experience?"

Dad waited for her response, and I could tell he was sweating a little. It took Mom four long swallows before she finally said, "Really, you would do that?"

"Of course I would, baby. Anything for you. I'll make it up to you, I promise," Dad said. And Mom grinned.

My father *was* good with the ladies, or at least he was good with my mother. When I got my first real girlfriend, I was going to ask him for advice. But right now, I had to deal with my fake one.

And at that moment the doorbell rang. I stopped chewing and stiffened.

Mom looked at me. "Aren't you going to get the door for your girlfriend?" she demanded. "I know I raised a gentleman."

I walked slowly to the door like I was heading

into the slammer. When I opened it, I immediately jumped back. Teresa had on a bright pink dress with two huge flowers on each shoulder. They looked like they were about to attack.

"Hi, Teresa. You look, uh, nice?" I greeted her, not sure what to say.

"Thanks, sweetie," she said, before giving me another wet kiss on my cheek. She strolled in like she was totally comfortable and gave my mom a big hug. I could see I was in trouble.

"Hi, everyone," said Teresa. "It's so good to see all of you. I feel like you're my second family."

So she could sit next to me, Drew gave up his seat and took the empty chair next to my father.

"Are you and Chris boyfriend and girlfriend?" Tonya asked.

Teresa smiled brightly. "Yes. Oh, Chris told you. I wanted us to tell your family together, honey." All the "honeys" and "sweeties" were making me really uncomfortable. She pinched my cheek hard and I flinched. She was freakishly strong.

Teresa looked at Tonya and commented, "You know, that means we're sisters."

And then, lo and behold, Tonya got up and hugged Teresa! "I always wanted a sister," she said.

How did Teresa manage to get Tonya on her side for free? I had never seen my sister willingly do something without getting some sort of cut.

"Teresa, I hope you're hungry," said my mother. "We've got plenty of food."

I looked at my father. He was shifting in his seat and carefully watching how much food my mother put on Teresa's plate.

"So, Teresa, your mother didn't cook?" he asked.

"She did, but I knew Chris wanted me to have our first family dinner together at his house," Teresa replied sweetly.

My father frowned at me. I knew he was mad, but I simply shrugged my shoulders. It was all I could do, as things were beyond my control.

At least his mood changed the next second when Teresa said, "Mr. Rock, I see where Chris gets his good looks."

Part of me wanted to yell, "Dad, don't fall for it," but part of me also didn't want him to be mad at me.

"Why, thank you, Teresa, I did raise two fine young men," my father answered, grinning like he'd just won the lottery. And all of a sudden it was cool for Teresa to be sitting at our table, eating our food. That girl had some weird power. She had my mom and dad eating out of her hands!

"Did Chris tell you all how he saved my life today?" asked Teresa. Uh-oh, here it comes.

"No, he didn't," my mother said, looking at me. "How did he do that?"

"Chris, you are so modest. Tell them how you defeated that mean boy, Joey."

"You beat up Joey?" Drew asked in disbelief.

"Well, I didn't exactly—"

"Oh, Chris, he was on the floor," Teresa added.

"And Drew, Chris told me that you're just as brave as he is. Strong men do run in the Rock family, huh?" Teresa told Drew, whose wide grin made it clear that he had gone over to enemy territory. I was now alone in my own family.

"You got in a fight in school today?" asked my mother, her voice full of concern. "You better not have gotten into trouble. I don't want to hear about you getting kicked out of that good school. And I'm not having any of my children go to jail. I'm not raising any criminals."

That's my mother's biggest fear: that one of her kids will end up in jail. Not that Drew and I were headed that way. I'm not sure about Tonya, though.

"No, Mom, it wasn't a fight, it was a small misunderstanding," I reassured her.

"Show them. Show them how you saved me," Teresa urged.

"Yeah, Chris, show us," said Tonya, with a sly look on her face.

"I'd like to see that," Drew added.

I had no choice but to reenact the morning's fake fight. Okay, I made some parts sound a little better.

I made Joey into a savage attacker who backed down in fear of my retaliations. I emerged as the courageous hero. I ended my performance with, "And if you ever bother Teresa again, you'll have to answer to me!" I smoothed my clothes like I'd seen Shaft do, and held my arm out for Teresa to grab. It felt good.

"Wow, son, you protected Teresa like that? That's so sweet," Mom declared, impressed. "I remember when your father used to do nice stuff like that for me."

"What do you mean?" asked Dad. "I'm always sticking up for you. How about the time when that meter maid was trying to give you a parking ticket?

I ran out of the house in my pajamas and talked her out of it."

"Julius, you were the one who parked the car there, not me," my mother replied. The look on her face made it clear that he needed to think of something better.

Dad was stumped for a second. Then he recalled, "What about the time I came to your job and told your boss to stop making you work all those late hours?"

"You just wanted me home to cook dinner early. And need I remind you that he fired me after you did that?" My mother was getting worked up. Maybe my father wasn't so good with the ladies after all. Or maybe the ladies were just too hard to please.

Over sweet-potato pie, Teresa and my mother launched into a discussion about our future together. I wanted to sink under the table and hide.

My father didn't even help me out in all the

madness. He didn't say a word. I think he was trying to come up with ways to make peace with my mother. He also made sure we all cleaned our plates.

"Wow, bro, you're sitting next to your future wife," Drew said. He found Mom's plans amusing. I found them horrifying, like a very bad scary movie where Teresa turned out to be a vampire that wanted to suck every ounce of my blood.

"I want to spend every moment of my free time with you," Teresa told me. I almost choked on my pie. "Tomorrow I need you to go with me somewhere."

"Oh, I can't, because I told Greg I would go over to his house," I quickly replied—and I wasn't lying! Greg and I had plans to play video games after school.

"Oh, Chris, you see Greg all the time," my mother said. "Teresa needs you."

And that settled it.

Chapter 4

The next day in school, I couldn't wait to pour out my troubles to Greg.

"On the bus this morning, Teresa spent one hour talking about her feelings, and the other hour telling me about her headband collection," I told him as we walked to class.

"Girls collect headbands?" Greg asked.

"Apparently so," I responded.

"Maybe I should buy some and give them as

presents to get dates," he said.

I ignored him and continued, "I wanted to jump off the bus and walk the rest of the way."

"I'm sure it wasn't that bad," said Greg. "Look, you've got a cute girl digging you, and all you can do is complain. If I were in your shoes, that's the last thing I'd be doing."

Greg wasn't sympathetic at all, so I tried to convince him that he was wrong. "She invited herself to dinner last night! She and my mother planned out the rest of our lives together! They decided that we're going to have three kids!"

"You? A father? Now that's funny. As many times as you've lost your little sister, I wouldn't trust you with my kids."

"I wouldn't either! Do you see my pain?" Clearly he didn't. And then I remembered, "Oh, and I can't come over your house today, because I have to be somewhere with Teresa."

Suddenly Greg's smirk turned into a frown.

"Whoa, I didn't know she was running you like that. She's cutting into our video game time! By the time she's done with you, we won't ever be able to hang out."

"That is what I've been trying to tell you!"

"Dude, you've got to do something. She'll ruin our friendship!" Greg exclaimed. Now he was starting to sound desperate.

○ ○ ○

During English class, we had to work in teams to revise the essays we'd written about our families.

My partner, Kimberly Livingston, was an overly enthusiastic reporter for the school newspaper and therefore thought she was an expert on writing. I didn't think my essay was award-winning, but it wasn't trash, either.

"Chris, your use of narrative is compelling but problematic at the same time," Kimberly told me.

"Okay," I said, even though I wasn't sure what she was talking about. "What parts are problematic?"

"I don't believe that someone can be so cheap." She was referring to my father. I hadn't intentionally painted him as cheap, but I did mention how he cuts stamps off the mail to try to reuse them.

"And little girls just don't bribe people this way." She didn't believe that my sister, Tonya, was so good at it.

"And you made Bed-Stuy seem like a good neighborhood, when we both know it's the inner city."

"This is all true, though," I told her. "I didn't make any of it up, and I actually live in a pretty normal neighborhood."

"Sure you do," Kimberly said, as she patted my hand before lowering her voice. "Chris, it's okay to be ashamed, but you shouldn't lie or make things up." She must have read a different essay. And she hadn't heard a word I said.

While Kimberly was telling me ways to make my essay more authentic, I looked up to see Teresa and the guidance counselor, Mr. Wright, talking to my English teacher. Yikes. This was not good. Teresa gave me a wave and then frowned at Kimberly.

"Class, we have a new student, Teresa Johnson. Can a group volunteer to include her and get her up to speed on what we're doing?" asked Mr. Gordon.

Then I remembered what Teresa had said this morning: "It's a shame we don't have any classes together. We need to do something about that."

Now I was scared. Teresa was looking more and more like a witch. I looked at Teresa, then at Kimberly, then at Mr. Gordon and Mr. Wright, before looking at Teresa again. I knew what I had to do. I just didn't want to do it.

Teresa put her hand on her hip. Very slowly I put up my hand.

"Great, thanks, Chris and Kimberly," Mr. Gordon said, sounding a little relieved. Teresa sprinted over like a track star.

"What took you so long, silly?" Teresa asked.

"Uh, Teresa, this is Kimberly," I said.

"Hi, Teresa, nice to meet you," said Kimberly.

Teresa didn't respond, and she had this suspicious look on her face. She pulled up a seat next to me. Actually, if she was any closer she would have been sitting on my lap.

"So how did you two end up working together?" she asked in a serious tone.

"Mr. Gordon assigned the groups," I said quickly.

"Really. Well, Kimberly, did Chris tell you that he's my boyfriend?"

Kimberly shrugged. She was too caught up in making sure I accurately captured the essence of the ghetto in my essay to notice Teresa's attitude.

"That's nice," she replied.

"Yes, we are very much in love," Teresa added.

I looked at the window to see if I could possibly jump out of it. Now we were in love? I had to do something, before . . . well, it was already too late.

O O O

While Greg and I were in the lunch line, Teresa came over.

"I don't have any extra money," I said quickly.

"That's okay, sweetie. I already bought my lunch. But I wanted to make sure you're coming to sit with me and some of my new friends."

She pointed to a table full of females that, under normal conditions, I'd be happy to sit with.

"Are you sure?" I asked her. After her treatment of Kimberly, I wasn't sure if I was allowed to be within fifty feet of other girls.

"Of course, why wouldn't I be?" she said with a smile.

I looked at Greg and he had a huge grin on his face. All he could think about was which one of them he was going to talk to first. I knew I had to take one for the team.

"Okay, we'll be over," I murmured.

So while Greg chatted with Christina, I listened

as Teresa and the rest of the girls planned our first date, which they determined would be on Friday. I was supposed to take her to a superfancy restaurant, like Armando's, the Italian place that my father took my mother to only on her birthday, because they didn't give out coupons.

I looked away and spotted Joey Caruso. Strangely, I hadn't seen him since yesterday's fake fight. I knew he hadn't forgotten how badly I'd embarrassed him—and I hadn't forgotten about the butt-kicking waiting for me.

And at that very moment, an idea popped into my head. Maybe I could kill two problems with one whipping. I got up from the table and walked over to Joey. I took a deep breath and purposely bumped into him. Joey turned around, and his face was redder than his hair.

I looked over to make sure Teresa was watching.

I figured if Teresa saw me get beat up, she'd break up with me for being so weak. She'd know that I wasn't a Prince Charming. I threw in a few words to get Joey.

"Let's settle this once and for all. Whoever wins this fight gets Teresa," I said as bravely as I could. I closed my eyes and braced myself for a hard punch.

But nothing happened.

I opened one eye and saw Joey staring at me.

"Did you hear what I said?" I repeated, this time louder. The whole cafeteria was staring at us.

Again Joey did nothing except look at me fiercely. Then he turned and walked away, just like that! I was sure I had entered the Twilight Zone.

Teresa ran up and squeezed the life out of me for the second time.

"Oh, Chris, you defeated him in my honor," she gushed. "He's scared of you, my big strong man." The lunchroom cheered like they'd just watched *The Return of Black Superman*, starring me.

Something was really wrong with this picture.

O   O   O

I didn't expect my plan in the cafeteria to backfire, but Joey's unusual behavior left me feeling like my whole world had been turned upside down. Why wasn't he playing his bully role? Why was he letting me embarrass him?

I found Joey at his locker. Carefully I tapped him on the shoulder.

"Why didn't you fight me?" I asked.

Before he could respond or use my body for wrestling practice, Mr. Carver, the principal, walked by and warned, "I'm watching you, Mr. Caruso. You're still on probation."

And there was my answer. Joey couldn't get into any more trouble right now or he'd be thrown out of school. I couldn't even get myself beat up!

Chapter 5

On the bus ride home, Teresa couldn't stop talking about my bravery during lunchtime. It was déjà vu.

"I can see us being together for a very long time," she declared, and pecked me on the cheek. I never would have thought I'd get tired of being kissed by a girl.

"Thanks for coming with me to my appointment today," she said.

Did I really have a choice? I wondered.

During the rest of the bus ride and even as we walked through Bed-Stuy, so many questions were running through my head that I didn't pay attention to where we were going. Why didn't I feel better about not getting beat up by Joey? How was I going to get out of this date on Friday? How was I going to get out of this relationship?

"We're here," Teresa told me, snapping me out of my deep thought.

My eyes nearly popped out of their sockets as I read the sign: MISS PAULETTE'S PRESS & CURL HAIR SALON. BEAUTY'S NEXT TO GODLINESS, AND GOD DON'T LIKE UGLY.

A hair salon? Teresa never mentioned that! Suddenly I broke out in a cold sweat. Teresa tried to grab my clammy hand, but I wouldn't budge. This was the one place my father had told me to never enter, under *any* circumstances. He called it a "hostile environment" for males. "Son," he said, "women in the hair salon will eat you alive. Take my word for it. Stay away!"

"Come on, sweetie, I'm already late for my hair appointment," Teresa said, pulling me.

"Uh, I don't think it's a good idea for me to go in there."

"Why?"

"Because it's for women. I'm not welcome in there."

"You are being so silly," Teresa gently scolded, and pulled on my hand so strongly that I stumbled behind her—and into the salon. Instantly it felt like a thousand scrutinizing eyes were glaring at me.

"Hi, ladies," Teresa announced. "This is my boyfriend, Chris."

No one responded. Women of all ages, including a little girl in a baby stroller, looked me up and down like I was a criminal—which might have been appropriate, because I felt like I was in jail.

"Teresa, you know the rules, no guests unless they're getting serviced," said a large woman with pink rollers.

"I know, Miss Paulette, but I wanted everyone to meet Chris. He's the one I've been talking about all these years."

The room made a collective moan.

"He's scrawnier than I imagined," Miss Paulette commented.

I stood motionless. I was on display, and it was about as fun as hiding behind garbage cans. I wondered if I dared to make a run for it.

"Well, tell him not to bother nothing," said Miss Paulette. "He's got to sit up front so Miss Alameda can watch him to make sure he don't take nothing."

"Thanks, Miss Paulette," Teresa chirped excitedly. She pointed to two plastic chairs. "Chris, I am going to get my hair washed, so you'll have to sit up front here. There are plenty of magazines for you to read. I won't take long, promise." She gave me another kiss on the cheek.

I looked at Miss Paulette. She had a disapproving

frown on her face. She was a scary-looking woman who could probably beat me far worse than Joey Caruso could. I didn't want to upset her, so I took a seat. This was the time to be seen and not heard, although I wished I didn't have to be seen, either. The women's stares were piercing holes into me.

To avoid their stares, I focused on the walls. The salon looked almost as old as Miss Paulette. The white paint had turned yellow. The floor was stained and cracked and covered with hair. There were posters on the walls of women with hairdos that resembled intricate puzzles. For a place that was selling beauty, it sure wasn't that attractive.

Miss Alameda stared at me the entire time I was up front. She reminded me of the mean old lady at the end of the block who always accused me of stealing her newspaper. I smiled at her, but she just stared back. I should have listened to my father.

Two women approached me. They looked to be my mother's age; one was taller than my father and

44

the other shorter than Tonya.

"What are your intentions with our Teresa?" the shorter woman asked.

They made me so nervous that all I managed to blurt out was, "Uh."

"You mean you don't know?" the tall one asked.

"Figures," said the short one.

"Well, we'll tell you what you won't do," the two women said in unison. How did they do that?

"You will not disrespect her," said the short woman.

"You will not be fresh with her," the taller woman added.

"That's right," agreed the shorter one.

I wanted to say, "Trust me, you don't have to worry about that," but I figured it was best to keep my mouth shut.

"Are you paying attention?" they asked, again in unison.

"Yes, ma'am, I mean, ma'ams."

"And you will not—listen good to this—*you will not break her heart*," the tall one declared.

A cold shiver went down my back. They looked like they could put a hit out on me.

"Do you understand?" they asked.

"Yes, yes, I understand," I said nervously.

I looked over at Teresa and she grinned. I was mad that she'd left me alone to be harassed. Why was she trying to make my life miserable?

I decided to look busy by reading a magazine. I looked at the selections, and all I saw were copies of *Essence* lying around. My mother had a subscription, and every time she read a new issue she had a "talk" with my father. I didn't think it was a good idea for me to read it, especially in the salon. I might learn things that I shouldn't know. I decided to take out my history textbook and read about a less combative subject: the Spanish-American War.

Chapter 6

Almost three hours passed before Teresa was finally finished. I was beyond exhausted. I didn't want to speak to her. I just wanted to get home.

"Miss Octavia and Miss Henrietta said they really liked you," she told me.

"Uh-huh," I said. What I really wanted to say was, "They didn't act like it when they were interrogating me."

We walked the rest of the way to her house in

silence. After I dropped her off, I rushed home. My mother was probably worried. She usually gives us only two minutes to be late before she started hunting us down. And I had missed dinner.

But when I got home, my mother was calmly sitting in the living room, reading the new issue of *Essence*. Apparently Teresa had already told her where we were going, as the first words out of her mouth were, "How was the hair salon?"

"Mom, I don't ever want to step foot into another one for the rest of my life."

She laughed and told me that I was being a great boyfriend to Teresa. Then she started reminiscing again about when she and my father first started dating.

"You know, your father used to go with me everywhere too when we first started going out. He didn't want to be away from me for even a second. He used to take me out all the time too. We would go for hot dogs and walk around the park. Or we would have dinner at his parents' house. It was so nice.

"He used to compliment me all the time, tell me how pretty I was," Mom added, her voice slowly hardening. Now she was getting mad. "Boy, you better treat Teresa like a queen."

I gulped. It was confirmed. I had no choice. I couldn't break up with Teresa because I'd have to face my mother. I'd have to make Teresa break up with me.

Mom suddenly perked up. "Oh, and Teresa told me that you two are going shopping tomorrow for a shirt for her to wear on your date on Friday," she said. "Don't worry, I'll be here to watch Drew and Tonya. Have fun."

"Right. Thanks," I said, resisting the urge to bang my head against the wall.

After I ate the dinner my mother had saved for me, I went to my room. On the way there, I stopped into Drew's room to see what type of women advice he could offer.

He was reading a copy of *Essence*.

"Hey, bro," he said, looking up.

"Why are you reading that?" I asked. "It's for girls."

"That's exactly why I'm reading it," replied my wise younger brother. "It gives me insight into how females think. You should read it sometime."

"No, thank you," I said quickly.

"Suit yourself. So what's up?" Drew asked.

"Uh, nothing. Well, not nothing. Okay, I'll spit it out. I need advice about Teresa."

"Oh, that's it? No problem. What's going on?"

"Well, how can I put it? This relationship is not what I expected. It requires a lot of time and energy. And I am not sure if I'm ready for all the commitment."

"So you want to break up with her," he said, as if he read my mind.

"Yes, but I don't want to hurt her feelings. I wonder if there's a way that I can get her to break up with me. Make it look like it was her idea, you know."

Drew took a deep breath. "Bro, let me tell you one thing. When it comes to breaking up with a female, you have to be a man about it. Be honest with Teresa and tell her that you're not ready for a relationship right now, but you want to remain friends."

Drew said this like he does it all the time. Girls probably accept it and are happy just to be his friend. But I knew Teresa wouldn't go for it.

"I don't think that's a good idea," I said.

"Trust me, honesty is the way to go with this one," Drew insisted. "She'll respect you, and it won't ruin your reputation with the other ladies."

"What do you say when you want to break up with someone?" I asked.

"Okay, you be Teresa and I'll be myself," Drew said.

"Why can't you be me?" I asked.

"I'm me because I'm showing you how I do it.

But if you want me to be you, fine," he said with a sigh. "Okay, first you take her by the hand." Drew reached for mine and I pulled it away quickly.

"What?" he asked.

"Do we have to really act it out?" I wanted to know.

"Do you want me to help you or not?"

I had no choice. "Fine." I held out my hand.

Drew picked up my hand as though he were picking up a newborn chick. "Then you look into her eyes," he said as he gazed into my eyes.

"Teresa, I really care about you. I think you are a really sweet girl." Holding my hand, Drew walked me over to his bed and sat me down.

"Lately I've been feeling that maybe this relationship is too much for me right now. You're so perfect, and well, I feel like I'm not good enough to make you happy." He put his arm around me.

"At this point, Teresa is most likely to say something like, 'But Chris, you do make me happy,' or

'That's not true, you *are* good enough.'"

Wow, maybe I should read *Essence*. My brother sure seemed to know what he as talking about. "How do I respond?" I asked, eager to know.

"You say, 'See, that's what I'm talking about, you're so sweet. And for that I will always deeply care for you. But right now I think it's best that we be friends. I don't want to hold you back from the happiness that you deserve.'" He rubbed my hand, and for some odd reason, I felt comforted.

Then I snapped out of it. "That will never work with Teresa. She'll just try to convince me that our relationship will work and last forever."

"It works on all females, trust me," Drew said. "You just have to stand your ground, but in a consoling kind of way."

I wasn't buying it. Although he had much more experience in dealing with girls, I wasn't about to be the one to break up with Teresa. That would be asking for trouble.

Chapter 7

"So how's married life?" Greg asked me while he took books out of his locker.

"Very funny," I replied. "Yesterday was the hair salon. Today we're going shopping for blouses. Being a boyfriend is exhausting."

"Hey, you said you'd come over today since you couldn't yesterday," Greg said. "I don't want to play Defender by myself."

"I know, I'm trying to come up with a plan.

Trust me, I'm working on it," I replied.

Just then Teresa snuck up behind me. "Hey, sweetie," she said.

"Oh, hey, you're here," I replied, hoping she hadn't heard me.

"You told Greg you're working on something. What are you working on?" she asked.

"Oh, uh . . . " I racked my brains for a perfect lie. Before I could answer, she guessed, "Are you working on plans for Friday?"

"Friday?" I asked.

"Yes, silly. Our first date."

"Uh, yeah, that's *exactly* what I'm working on," I said, relieved.

"I knew it!" she exclaimed excitedly. "You're going to surprise me, right? Oh, I can't wait!" She gave me a hug before skipping away.

That was way too close. "You didn't help me out," I accused Greg.

"What did you want me to say?" Greg asked.

"She caught me off guard. She came out of nowhere."

"Yeah, she does that," I replied.

"Friday's the big day? You should make it the worst date ever, I bet that would get her to break up with you," he said, joking.

Suddenly a lightbulb the size of a basketball went off in my head. "That's it! Greg, you're a genius. I could kiss you!" I shouted, jumping up and down.

Greg looked stricken. "Please don't," he said. "Just because you don't want a girlfriend doesn't mean I don't either."

"I'll sabotage our date by acting like a fool," I decided, feeling like I had control over my life for the first time in days. "That shouldn't be too hard. I'm good at that."

Greg nodded his head. "It's definitely better than trying to get yourself beat up by Joey Caruso. Did I tell you how stupid that was?"

Teresa wanted to go blouse shopping in an upscale clothing store in the "nice part" of Brooklyn. We entered, and the security guard immediately gave me a strange look, one that told me I'd better watch my step. I knew at any moment he would start following us. I walked with my hands on my shoulders so he could see them. I also announced everything I was about to do, like, "I'm about to touch this shirt," or "I am holding this pair of pants up to me to see if they would fit."

Teresa went to the girls' section and started picking out blouses and asking me for my opinion.

"What do you think of this one?" It was bright orange, with yellow polka dots and lots of frills. It was pretty awful-looking.

"Nice?" I ventured, not knowing what to say.

"Okay, what about this one?" It was neon blue and had a big bow on the front.

"Pretty?"

Teresa must have looked at every blouse in the

section. She picked each one up and asked me what I thought. I told her that every single one was either "nice," "pretty," or "interesting." And she piled most of them into my arms. I looked over at the security guard. He hadn't taken his eyes off of me.

Now I understood why my father gave my mother money and told her to have fun. Females have too many clothes to choose from. I'd never seen so many blouses in my life. And they all looked alike, just with different colors!

Teresa decided to try on each blouse. I would have protested, but it meant that I could finally sit down. I took a seat outside the dressing room with a mountain of shirts on my lap. Then she came out and modeled each one by spinning around and posing with her hand on her hip. Then she'd wait for my response, which was always, "Looks nice on you."

After tons of spins, I felt dizzy, but she was finally finished. She had two blouses in her hands.

I wondered how she was going to pay for them. They were twenty-five dollars each.

"How can you afford them?" I asked. I hoped she wasn't going to tell me to pay for them, because I surely didn't have any money.

"Oh, I'm not going to buy them," she answered matter-of-factly.

Oh, no. Did I have a thief on my hands? I couldn't go to jail. Mom would kill me.

"I can't afford this stuff," Teresa explained. "I come here to see what kind of shirt I want, and then I go home and draw it out for my mother. She'll sew one just like it."

Well, that's creative, but didn't we just spend two whole hours searching for a shirt that she wasn't going to buy? I could have been playing video games with Greg!

Teresa put the two shirts back. I kept my hands on my shoulders as we walked past the security guard, then loudly announced that I was leaving.

Chapter 8

During English the next day, Teresa kept passing me notes that said things like, "Guess who loves you," to which I replied, "My mom?" Then she would write back, "I love your sense of humor. You should be a comedian."

Her next note, however, put fear in my heart. It read: "I forgot to tell you. My mother wants to talk to you before you take me out tomorrow. So you'll have to come over today."

I'd met Miss Jackie before, but this time the circumstances were different. Boyfriend circumstances. There was no telling how she'd react to me. And if the response at the hair salon was any indicator, tonight was going to be a nightmare.

I sent Teresa a note back to see if she knew what her mother might want to talk about. She replied, "I'm sure it's nothing, sweetie." This note included an extra-big heart shape.

She told me the same day on purpose, so that I couldn't try to get out of seeing her mom! Now I couldn't even prepare myself, to try to get advice from Drew or fake sick.

For the rest of the day, I tried unsuccessfully to avoid Teresa. I really wished Corleone had garbage cans in the hallway for me to hide behind.

On the way home, I tried again to find out why Miss Jackie wanted to see me.

"Well, she hasn't seen you since we became boyfriend and girlfriend. I know she was wondering why you didn't ask her permission first."

Huh? Probably because it wasn't my idea in the first place! But I couldn't say that. Instead I asked, "Is she mad?"

"No, honey," Teresa replied. "You know my mother, she is the sweetest woman I know, next to Miss Paulette."

I put my head down. I was doomed.

When we arrived at Teresa's house, Miss Jackie, who had raised Teresa by herself since her husband died, was changing the lightbulb on the porch light.

"Hi, Mommy," Teresa said as she gave her a big hug.

"Hey, baby, how was school?" asked her mother.

"It was good. I brought Chris over to talk to you."

"Chris, it is so good to see you. I think you were a foot shorter the last time I saw you. You are growing into such a nice-looking young man."

I blushed. She gave me a hug, too. Maybe this wasn't going to be bad after all.

"Are you hungry? I have some leftovers from yesterday."

I knew my mother would be mad if she heard I'd eaten elsewhere, as it made her think I didn't like her food, so I said, "No, thank you. I'm fine."

"Okay, well, do you mind helping me with something?" she asked.

"I'll be right back," Teresa said and went into the house. I didn't realize then how convenient her exit was.

"No, I don't mind," I told Miss Jackie. "Do you need help with the lightbulb?"

She smiled. "Aren't you a sweetheart? That's why my Teresa likes you so much."

Then she walked over and grabbed a rake and a garbage bag. "I just need you to rake these leaves in the back and the front."

I looked at the lawn. It was completely covered with leaves. It would take me hours to finish raking it!

"Let me know when you're finished out here and I'll take you around back," she instructed, handing me the rake before going inside. Suddenly she wasn't so nice anymore.

I wanted to cry, although I knew the idea of shedding tears because I had a girlfriend was a crazy one. But this wasn't how I'd imagine my first girlfriend to be. Firstly, it would be with someone that I really liked. I imagined us going roller-skating and getting pizza. Not going to hair salons and fancy boutiques—or doing manual labor!

I took a deep breath and began. The rake was old and half-broken. It made my task much harder than it had to be. After a while, Teresa came out with cookies she had baked for me.

She stayed outside to watch me, although she never offered to help. I was finally done with the front, and Teresa walked me around to the backyard. I wanted to scream. If the front was covered in leaves, the back was *buried*. Teresa had set me up big-time. I wondered if the whole boyfriend thing was just a big conspiracy to get some unsuspecting fool (me) to rake their leaves for free.

After about three hours, I was almost finished, and I was exhausted. When Teresa saw that I had only a corner left, she asked, "You know what would be romantic?"

"No," I said with a sigh.

"If you raked a heart out of the leaves for me."

○   ○   ○

When I finally got home, I had leaves in my hair, on my clothes, and in my shoes. I never knew how bad wet leaves really smelled. My mother made me jump into the shower immediately. She told me that I wasn't going to stink up her entire house.

Later that night I went to my father for advice. I couldn't take the relationship any longer. Being a boyfriend was like a full-time job that I wasn't getting paid for. I wondered if all relationships were like this.

My dad was in his bedroom clipping his toenails.

"Dad, I need some advice about women." He looked up from his feet and seemed happy that I'd asked him.

"Well, son," he said, motioning for me to sit next to him. "Relationships are complicated. Women are complicated. It's good that you learn that early. You'll be much better off. Take your mother, for instance. She's mad at me for a bad date that happened years ago. Now, I could fight with her about it. But that wouldn't be smart. Instead I'm just going to make it up to her by taking her on that second first date on Friday."

"Tomorrow?" I asked.

"Yep. I'm going to take her to Armando's, you know, that fancy Italian place? And it's not even her birthday. She'll be so surprised. Son, that's how you accumulate what we men call cool points."

My mind was racing.

"Why was your first date so bad?" I inquired.

"Oh, it was embarrassing. I remember it like it was yesterday. Your mother had turned me down for a date, like, three times before she finally agreed to go out with me. She was so beautiful, and I was just a skinny teenager with a big head and no money. Needless to say, I was nervous. I took her to a pizza place where my friend worked. He hooked us up with two large pies. Things weren't going too well. I was so nervous that I didn't talk that much. Instead I ate and ate and ate. I ate until I was so sick that I threw up at the table! Luckily, none of it got on your mother. But she was still so mad that she didn't talk to me for weeks. It was terrible."

"That sounds really awful," I said, as my plan to get rid of Teresa firmly took root.

Chapter 9

I woke up the next morning with renewed energy. It was D-Day—Date Day—and hopefully, by the end of it, life would be back to normal. I didn't care that Tonya took nearly an hour in the bathroom to get dressed, or that Drew ate the last of the French toast.

On the way to school, I told Teresa how excited I was about our date. It wasn't a complete lie. I was excited that the date would mean the end of me being her boyfriend. I asked her if her mom had sewn the blouse. She said it wasn't ready yet and she'd decided to wear a dress instead. For a moment I thought about all the time we spent in that store looking for "the perfect blouse," but I didn't dwell on it. I told her that since I was going to take her to a fancy restaurant, her nicest dress would be appropriate.

She was thrilled and told me that our first date would definitely be unforgettable. I couldn't have agreed more.

When I got to school, I pulled Greg into the bathroom.

"Why did you drag me in here?" he asked.

"Because I can't risk Teresa sneaking up on us. I need to talk to you about my plan for tonight. I even came up with a name for it. I call it Operation R.O.O.T."

"What does that stand for?"

"It stands for Rid Ourselves of Teresa. What do

you think? Pretty clever, huh?"

"Yeah, I guess so. It's too bad she's such a pain," he said, shaking his head. "We dreamed about the day we would have girlfriends, not the day we were plotting to break up with one. So what's your plan?"

I quickly told Greg my plan, and he gave me a few ideas to make it even better. "If that doesn't make her want to stop speaking to you, I don't know what will!"

Then we headed to class, after spending way too much time in the boys' bathroom. Guys were beginning to look at us funny.

For the rest of the day, I was the perfect boyfriend to Teresa. I didn't want her to suspect anything.

I also saw Caruso a couple of times, and he just walked right past. No elbows to my stomach, no jokes about my outfit. Nothing. Life was good.

When three o'clock came around, Greg wished

me luck. "Well, this will be the end, huh?"

"Yep," I replied, nodding.

"I'm going to miss her always around us," he said. I couldn't tell if he was serious or not.

"*You* can always be her boyfriend, you know," I joked.

"No, that's okay. She's too much woman for me," Greg answered with a grin.

O O O

When I got home, I immediately launched Operation R.O.O.T. and looked for my mother. She was in her room trying on clothes for her big date with Dad.

"You look very pretty," I said, and I meant it too.

"Thank you, son. You know, I've had this dress for almost a year now, and this is the first time I've been able to wear it." She smiled and did a spin.

I hadn't seen my mother this excited in a while, which made me feel bad for what I was about to do—but I had to keep my mind on the bigger picture.

"Teresa is wearing a special dress tonight as well."

"Ohhh! My baby is growing up into a young man and going on his first date. Are you nervous?"

I sort of nodded before asking, "I was thinking, wouldn't it be nice if Teresa and I joined you and Dad tonight?"

My mother stopped looking at herself in the mirror and gave me that boy-what-are-you-up-to look.

"I mean, I guess I am really nervous, and I thought that with you and Dad there, I would feel better and not mess things up."

She gave me the eye squint. I couldn't believe I was lying to my mother and hoping she'd go along with it.

"I don't know, Chris. This is a chance for your

father and me to be alone," she said.

"I mean, we don't have to sit with you two. We can sit where you can't even see us. I just thought it would be nice, um, knowing that you were close by, for advice."

She thought about it. I gave her the most pathetic look that I could muster.

"Well, I guess so," she finally said. "You just better be on your best behavior. Don't embarrass me by acting like a fool."

I gave my mother a hug so I didn't need to open my mouth and tell another lie. I knew that by the end of the evening, she was going to be totally embarrassed.

So step one of Operation R.O.O.T. was successful. Teresa would be upset when she found out that we weren't going out alone. That's all she had been talking about, having me to herself. Maybe she'd break up with me right then and there and I wouldn't have to go through with the rest of my plan. But I knew that was just wishful thinking.

On to step two, which I knew would be easier than the first. I went into Tonya's room. She was combing the hair of a big-headed doll.

"Tonya, want to go out with Mom, Dad, Teresa, and me tonight?" I asked.

She looked up and said, "Mom said that Drew and I are going over Miss Josephine's."

"Do you want to go with us or not?"

"Did Mom say it was okay?"

"Not exactly, but if you want to go, I can arrange it. Then you don't have to go over Miss Josephine's. I know how boring it is over there."

"How are you going to arrange it?" Tonya was asking too many questions.

"Look, don't worry about it. I'll handle it."

"What are you going to give me?"

Here comes the bribery. Tonya is one of the best hustlers in all of Bed-Stuy.

"Give you? I'm helping you. Do you really want

to go to Miss Josephine's?" I asked.

She just stared at me.

"Fine, I'll buy you candy for an entire week."

"And?"

And? Now she was just being greedy.

"Okay . . . for two weeks."

She went back to combing her doll's hair with a smug look on her face. "Okay," she finally agreed.

I breathed a sigh of relief before going up to Drew, who was watching TV in the living room.

"I need a favor," I said, deciding to take the straightforward route with my brother.

"What is it?"

"I need you to tag along on my date with Teresa tonight."

"Are you breaking up with her?" he asked.

"Not exactly. She's going to break up with me. Well, that's what I'm planning for."

"Chris, I'm telling you, you should just be honest."

"I can't. She's got Mom on her side. I can't break up with her for no reason. Plus I don't want Teresa to like me anymore. I figure if she breaks up with me, she'll also stop liking me."

"What's your plan?" he asked.

I didn't want him to know all of Operation R.O.O.T., so I told him only what he needed to know in order to help me.

"I don't know if I can be a part of this," he said.

"Well, what if I clean your room for . . . two weeks? Will you help me?"

Drew's eyes lit up. Apparently I had made him an offer he couldn't refuse. "Okay, but I'm going to say 'I told you so,' when your plan blows up in your face."

I grinned as I headed downstairs. Just one more part of step two. It was already five o'clock, and I had to hurry up, as Teresa was coming over at six thirty.

I found my dad in the kitchen, eating so that he wouldn't have to buy a real meal at Armando's.

"Hey, Dad, I found these coupons for the Chicken Shack. Buy one meal and get one free. They expire today." I held up the coupons like they were Knicks tickets. I knew I didn't have to say anything else. My father couldn't let a coupon expire, no matter what.

Sure enough, he said, "How did I miss these? I can't let these good coupons go to waste. Your mother shouldn't care where I take her, right? It's the thought that counts."

Dad was trying to convince himself, and I was going to help him. "That's what you always tell me," I said.

"I'll just take her to Armando's for her birthday," he said decisively. "Tonight I'll take her to the Chicken Shack."

Chapter 10

I had the perfect outfit for my date with Teresa. It was a powder blue church suit that Drew outgrew a few years ago, and it was now even a couple of sizes too small for me. I pulled my black dress socks up to my knees and put on these white patent leather shoes that my mother loved but I hated. I looked at myself in the mirror and smiled. I looked absolutely ridiculous.

Teresa was ten minutes early, but I was ready.

When I came to the door, she tried to hide how she felt about my outfit.

"Hey, sweetie . . . wow, what an outfit," she said hesitantly.

"Yep, I wanted to dress up tonight. What do you think?"

"Uh, it's fine. But it looks a little small for you."

"Thanks, you look nice too," I replied. "That's a pretty dress." It really was a nice dress. Black with three white stripes at the bottom.

"Thank you, it's my favorite. I wanted to look extraspecial tonight."

My parents came downstairs, followed by Drew and Tonya, who burst out laughing when they saw my suit. I thought Drew wasn't going to recover.

My mother told them to stop and said that she was glad I was making use of "that good suit."

She walked over and gave Teresa a hug. "Hi, dear. You look so pretty."

"Thank you, Mrs. Rock," said Teresa as she did a little curtsy.

"I'm coming with you," Tonya told Teresa.

"No, I'm dropping them off at Miss Josephine's house," my mother said.

I cut in. "Uh, actually Mom, Drew and Tonya are coming with Teresa and me. We're making it a family affair."

My mother looked at me sideways. She was about to speak when my father interrupted.

"Rochelle, dear, we should get going. It's okay if the kids come, we won't sit near them. They won't bother us." He gave me a look. It was news to him that we were all going to dinner together, but I think he figured having us around would mean my mom would have less of a fit once she found out where he was taking her.

"Well, okay, honey," Mom said. "I'm letting you plan this date, and I know you are going to make sure it's perfect." Her you-better-or-else tone made my father start to scratch his neck, which meant he was nervous.

As we walked out the front door of the building, Drew pulled me aside. "You sure you want to go through with this?"

"I'm sure," I told him.

We piled into my father's truck. Teresa was squished between Tonya and me.

"I thought we were going alone," she whispered.

"Oh, no, my brother and sister go everywhere with me, especially on dates." Tonya and Drew smiled on cue. Teresa looked disappointed. Operation R.O.O.T. was coming together nicely.

We drove up to the Chicken Shack. Everyone was confused.

"Why are we here?" my mother asked.

"Well, dear, I found these coupons and—"

"Found coupons? You promised me a nice second first date. And you think I would be okay with coming to a greasy chicken place?"

"Yeah, Chris. I thought we were going to a fancy restaurant," Teresa chimed in.

"This is fancy," I responded. "Only the best chicken for you!"

"Honey, calm down," my father said. "We are still going to have a special date. It'll just be at a significant discount. It shouldn't matter where we go, as long as we're together." He grabbed my mother's hand and kissed it.

"Did I tell you how amazing you look tonight? You are wearing that dress," he added.

I was sure my mother wasn't going to fall for that. I might as well throw in the towel—Operation R.O.O.T. was ruined.

But she smiled. "I guess you're right, honey," she said.

Wow, my father was smooth after all.

"Your parents are so cute together. I hope we're like that when we get older," said Teresa.

"Let's go eat some greasy chicken," I replied.

Chapter 11

If there was one thing that the Chicken Shack was known for, it was their greasy chicken. That, and the horrible service, the dirty yellow life-size chicken in front of the door, and the fact that it really was the size of a shack but could somehow pack in a hundred people on a busy Sunday after church. Luckily, it wasn't too crowded this evening, just a few families getting take-out for dinner. Two of the four booths were available.

Teresa, Drew, Tonya, and I piled into one of them. I jumped in next to Drew, which forced Teresa to sit next to Tonya. My parents sat on the other side of the restaurant. But in the Chicken Shack that wasn't far away at all.

Quickly I motioned for Drew to start doing his part of our deal.

"Teresa, did you ever hear about the time Chris peed in the bed?" he asked.

I had told Drew to tell embarrassing stories about me, ones that would make Teresa rethink her "Prince Charming." I guess he decided to make them up.

Tonya burst out laughing.

"No, I haven't," Teresa said.

"Our mother put one of those rubber sheets on his bed. It's still there in case he has an accident." Drew was obviously getting a kick out of this.

"What about that time you cried after watching an episode of *Speed Racer*?" he said next.

"You cried?" Teresa asked.

"Yeah, *Speed Racer* always manages to get me choked up," I answered.

"Oh, really?" she said in that high-pitched voice. "That just means you're sensitive. See, there are so many reasons why I like you." She grabbed my cheek from across the table.

Tonya and Drew snickered. Well, that didn't work quite as I'd planned. It was time to move on to the next step: Act the fool.

"Hey, Teresa, did you know I could burp on cue?" I asked her.

I began burping the theme song to *Good Times*.

"Teresa, join in," I said.

"No, thank you. That's disgusting, Chris."

"It's one of my biggest talents. Any requests?"

"Yeah, do Billy Ocean," said Tonya.

I burped "Caribbean Queen" in its entirety. By the look on Teresa's face, my crudeness was working.

"Any other requests?"

"Chris, that's enough, really. I thought you and I were going to have a special time together."

"We are," I said. "I have a surprise for you. It's spitball time!" I folded up the wrapper from the straws and tried to hit Teresa.

"Stop, Chris," she said sternly.

Drew joined in and hit Tonya on the head. Tonya squealed, but fought back. We were having a full-blown spitball fight. My parents were too much into each other to hear us.

"Chris, this is pretty juvenile," Teresa complained, pouting.

I ignored the comment and rolled a big one just for her, but somehow I misfired. The spitball hit my mother!

My mother got up in a flash. "Boy, what is wrong with you?" she yelled. "Why are you acting like you don't have any home training? I know I raised you better than that!"

I immediately aborted this step. I took a deep

breath and calmly asked Teresa, "What would you like to eat? You can get anything you want."

"Don't they just sell chicken?" she said with a little irritation in her voice.

"Well, yeah, but you can get whatever piece of chicken you want. Breast, thigh, wing?"

"I'll take two wings, I guess," she said. It was clear that this was not the date she had envisioned.

"Okay, two wings it is," I told her, getting up to walk to the counter.

"What about us?" asked Tonya.

"What about you?"

"We're hungry," Drew said.

I didn't want Drew or Tonya to jeopardize things, so I agreed to get them a chicken box that they could share. I ordered two chicken boxes for myself. Buying all that chicken nearly cleaned out my savings.

Next step: Gross her out. I attacked my chicken like a lion attacks his prey. I ripped the wing apart and put the entire piece in my mouth. I chomped hard, grunting and slurping, and wiped my mouth with the back of my hand.

"Chris, why are you eating like that?" Teresa asked.

"What do you mean?"

"You're eating like you've never had a meal before."

"Nah, umf, I'm jus' hungry, I guess," I answered with a mouth full of food. A bit of food flew out of my mouth and landed on the table.

Everyone at the table was grossed out, myself included.

"Chris, this really isn't the type of date I was expecting," Teresa said. She was angry, but she was trying not to show it. "You're not acting like yourself. It's like you don't want to be here."

"What are you talking about?" I asked. "This is how I am. Are you saying you don't like it?"

"No, I don't like it," she said.

Tonya and Drew were suddenly quiet.

"Then you're saying you don't like me?" I asked, trying to get her to dump me.

"Chris, is there something you want to tell me?"

"Uh, are you going to eat that piece?" I asked her. It was time to launch my secret weapon.

Teresa looked at me like I was crazy and shook her head. I had already finished my two chicken boxes and gobbled her leftover wing. I was starting to feel queasy. I looked over at my parents' table and saw that my dad had a chicken thigh on his plate. I steadied myself as I walked over to their table.

"Dad, are you going to eat that?" I asked.

My father looked at me. "Well, of course I wasn't going to let it go to waste. You can have it," he said, handing me the piece.

I ate the thigh in about ten seconds flat. That's when the queasy feeling came back—hard. The Chicken Shack is known for the greasiest chicken in all of Brooklyn. It was a joke that the chicken was so good, it was worth the pain that occurred afterward. I knew that if I ate enough of it, I'd blow. And that was the plan.

My stomach did cartwheels and backflips. I couldn't hold all the chicken down. I felt like a volcano that was about to erupt. It was coming, coming, coming. I got up and let go. All the chicken I just ate landed on Teresa—in her hair, on her special dress, and on her shoes. She screamed like I had never heard a person scream before. And then she began crying uncontrollably.

It was complete chaos after that.

My mother yelled at me for throwing up and ruining her second first date. My father yelled at me for wasting his last piece of chicken. Tonya yelled at me because some of my vomit hit her. One of the Chicken Shack employees yelled at me because he had to clean up the mess.

Drew patted me on the back. "You should have

just been honest, bro," he said sadly.

"Come on, girls," my mother said, taking Teresa and Tonya into the bathroom to get cleaned up. They all gave me looks that made me want to take back the entire evening.

I felt terrible. My stomach was completely empty, but not in a good way. Dad was still ranting, so now I also had a horrible headache.

When Teresa came out of the bathroom, she had stopped crying. Her dress was stained and her hair was wet. She looked at me and said, "I *never* want to speak to you again."

I didn't know whether to feel happy or sad. Operation R.O.O.T. was a success, but I didn't feel as good as I thought I would. The ride home was completely silent. Dad's truck smelled like rotten eggs.

"Bye, Teresa," I said, as we dropped her off. She just slammed the door in my face.

Chapter 12

All weekend I felt terrible, like the Knicks had lost the NBA championship by one point. My mother was so mad. "Boy, I don't even want to see you right now," she'd say whenever I came into a room.

I knew that on Monday I'd have to apologize to Teresa for ruining the date. I had taken things too far. Just because I didn't want to be her boyfriend didn't mean she was a bad person or deserved what I did. Drew was actually right, I should have been honest. I could have avoided having my whole family mad at me.

My father spent the entire weekend in the doghouse. My mother blamed part of the nightmare date on him. I told her that it wasn't his fault, because I shouldn't have shown him the coupons. But she didn't want to hear it. Now my father had to do something to make up for two bad first dates.

Sunday night I dreamed that Teresa was so mad about what I did that she organized a plan of her own. She called it Operation Get Back at Chris for Breaking My Heart. When I went outside to walk to the bus, everyone from the hair salon was dressed in army fatigues. They threw hair rollers at me. Then Miss Paulette chased me with a hot comb, and despite her age, she was as fast as an Olympic sprinter. I ran like my life depended on it, because it did, but I fell over some garbage cans in the street. The women caught up with me and stood over me, chanting, "Get him back, get him back!" I was pleading, "No, no, I'm sorry. I'm really sorry." Miss Octavia and Miss Henrietta held me down, saying, "We told you not to break her heart." Teresa walked slowly toward me with a bucket of greasy chicken. In this really evil voice, she asked, "Are you hungry? Do you want some more chicken?"

I jumped out of bed, and for the rest of the night I couldn't sleep. I began rehearsing my apology speech.

At breakfast my mother still wasn't speaking to me. But I broke the silence and told her that I was going to apologize to Teresa.

"Oh, I know you are," was all she said.

When Teresa got on the bus, I called her name, but she ignored me and walked right past my seat. The two-hour ride was disturbingly quiet and extremely long without her sitting next to me.

When I got to school, Greg rushed up to me, eager to hear if Operation R.O.O.T. had worked. "So how'd it go? Are you free?"

"It was a success, all right," I said. "She said she never wants to speak to me ever again."

"Congrats, bud," he declared, holding his hand out. I didn't slap it.

"I took things too far," I continued. "I really hurt her feelings, and now I feel bad about it. Not to mention the fact that I ruined my parents' evening. Everyone is mad at me. It was horrible."

"That's too bad," Greg said sympathetically. "Maybe you should have just been honest with her." *Now* he was suggesting honesty.

Just then Teresa walked by, without even glancing my way.

"Wow," said Greg. "She really is giving you the cold shoulder." Then, when he saw the look on my face, he added, "Just give it time, dude. I'm sure she'll forgive you."

"I hope so," I said as I walked slowly to class.

During English I tried to pass her a note that said, "I'm sorry," but she raised her hand and told Mr.

Gordon that I was disturbing her learning process.

For the rest of the day, I thought about when I could apologize to Teresa. I decided I'd do it on the bus ride home. I'd corner her, force her to hear me out, beg for forgiveness, and hope that she would want to be friends.

On the way to the bus, I was practicing my apology speech when I felt a tap on my shoulder. I turned around. It was Joey and Teresa—together.

"Guess who's off probation?" sneered Joey. "You thought you could get away with throwing up on my new girlfriend? Now I have even more reason to terrorize you!"

After the relationship with me, Teresa had moved on.

"Get him, Joey," Teresa ordered with a devilish smile on her face.

I took one look at Joey and Teresa. Then I took off running.

Now things were really back to normal.